E
MC

McInnes, John

Have you ever seen
a monster?

		DATE		
NO 25 '75	NO 1 '78	MR 30 '83	JA 29 '85
DE 10 '75	JA 19 '79	MY 2 '83	FE 12 '85
1 6	OC 10 '79	MY 17 '83	T-7
MY 21 '76	NO 9 '79		AP 29 '85
T-5	T 9	JE 1 '83	MY 28 '85
DE 9 '76	MY 20 '81	OC 24 '83	T 9
JA 19 '77	NO 9 '81	NO 8 '83	9-96 K
OC 7 '77	MR 1 '82		12-97 K
NO 4 '77	T-7	DE 5 '83	3-99 K
NO 18 '77	JA 3 '83	NO 28 '8	3-00 K
T 5	FE 2 '83	JA 2 '85	K2-910
OC 18 '78	MR 14 '83	JA 2 '85	K2 2-02
		JA 16 '85	

Have you ever seen a
monster?
McInnes, John
E
NOT AR

© THE BAKER & TAYLOR CO.

Have You Ever
Seen a Monster?

Have You Ever
Seen a Monster?

By John McInnes

Drawings by Tom Eaton

GARRARD PUBLISHING COMPANY
CHAMPAIGN, ILLINOIS

Have You Ever Seen a Monster?

Have you ever
seen a monster
ride like this?

I saw one
do something better.

Have you ever
seen a monster
talk like this?

I saw one
do something better.

Have you ever
seen a monster
sail like this?

I saw one
do something better.

Have you ever
seen a monster
eat like this?

I saw one
do something better.

Have you ever
seen a monster
play like this?

I saw one
do something better.

Have you ever
seen a monster
wash like this?

I saw one
do something better.

Have you ever
seen a monster
hop like this?

I saw one
do something better.

Have you ever
seen a monster
paint like this?

I saw one
do something better.

Have you ever
seen a monster
go up and down like this?

I saw one
do something better.

Have you ever
seen a monster
sleep like this?

I saw one.
do something better.

Have you ever
seen a monster
walk like this?

ADRIAN PUBLIC SCHOOLS
Adrian, Michigan

I saw one
do something better.

Have you ever
seen a monster
ride like this?

I saw one
do something better.

Have you ever
seen a monster
fly like this?

I saw one
do something better.

Have you ever
seen a monster
slide like this?

I saw one
do something better.